Quinito's Neighborhood

El vecindario de Quinito

Story / Cuento
Ina Cumpiano

Illustrations / Ilustraciones
José Ramírez

Children's Book Press ◉ an imprint of Lee & Low Books Inc.
New York

My mami is a carpenter.
My papi is a nurse.

Mi mami es carpintera.
Mi papi es enfermero.

My abuela drives a big truck.
My abuelo fixes clocks.

Sometimes my abuela
brings broken grandfather clocks
to my abuelo's shop.

Mi abuela maneja
un camión bien grande.
Mi abuelo es relojero.

A veces mi abuela
lleva relojes de caja
que no funcionan
al taller de mi abuelo.

My tía is a muralist.
My tío teaches dance.

Mi tía es muralista.
Mi tío da clases de baile.

My grown-up cousin Tita goes to clown school.

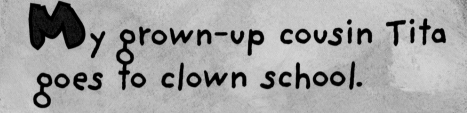

Mi prima Tita, que ya es grande, va a la escuela para ser payasa.

9

Her brother,
my primo Ruperto, is a dentist.
He checks people's teeth.

Su hermano,
mi primo Ruperto, es dentista.
Le examina los dientes
a la gente.

My neighbors,
Rafi and Luis Manuel,
go to work very early.
Rafi bakes bread
and Luis Manuel sells it.

Mis vecinos,
Rafi y Luis Manuel,
salen a trabajar
muy tempranito.

Rafi hace el pan
y Luis Manuel lo vende.

12

Mrs. Hernández sells Rafi's bread
at her bodega, too.
And her daughter, Sonia Isabel,
counts the money in the bank
on the corner.

La señora Hernández también vende el pan de Rafi en su bodega.

Y su hija, Sonia Isabel, cuenta dinero en el banco de la esquina.

Guillermo is our mailman.
Guillermo is going to marry
Sonia Isabel.

Guillermo es cartero.
Guillermo se va a casar
con Sonia Isabel.

Doña Estrella is a seamstress.
She is sewing a wedding dress
for Sonia Isabel.

Doña Estrella es costurera.
Le está cosiendo el traje de boda
a Sonia Isabel.

Mr. Gómez
is Doña Estrella's neighbor.
He is also my teacher at school.

Mrs. Gómez is a crossing guard.
She helps me cross the street.

El señor Gómez
es el vecino de Doña Estrella.
También es mi maestro.

La señora Gómez es la guardia escolar.
Me ayuda a cruzar la calle.

And I am a very busy person, too.
I have to tell Mr. Gómez
that my mami is a carpenter
and my papi is a nurse.

Y yo, también, soy una persona muy ocupada.
Le tengo que decir al señor Gómez
que mi mami es carpintera
y mi papi es enfermero.

the writer and the artist

Ina Cumpiano
is a Puerto Rican poet and translator who now lives in a busy, friendly neighborhood in San Francisco, California. As a teenager, she was a television actress, and she has since worked as a cashier, a teacher of languages and literature, and a free-lance writer and editor. She has published nearly twenty books for children. But her favorite job so far has been as a grandmother: she has ten grandchildren, ages two to thirteen.

For my five—Maya, Benjamin, Leah, Devin, and Kaitlyn, and for the five that are as good as mine—Jordan, Annabelle, Austin, Ezra, and Hugo. / Para mis cinco—Maya, Benjamin, Leah, Devin y Kaitlyn, y para los cinco que son casi míos— Jordan, Annabelle, Austin, Ezra y Hugo. —I.C.

José Ramírez
was born in Los Angeles, California. He is a gifted artist and also a second grade teacher for the Los Angeles Unified School District. His paintings, ceramic sculptures, and tile murals have been shown in museums, galleries, bookstores, coffee shops, and public spaces in the US and abroad. He has also conducted art workshops for museums, various community-based organizations, musician's groups, and after-school programs in and around Los Angeles, where he lives. This is his fourth book for children.

I dedicate this book to all the students I've taught and learned from over the past twelve years. / Dedico este libro a todos los estudiantes que he enseñado y de los cuales he aprendido durante los últimos doce años. —J.R.

words to know

abuelo - grandfather	primo - male cousin
abuela - grandmother	prima - female cousin
tío - uncle	bodega - small neighborhood grocery store
tía - aunt	

Children's Book Press
is an imprint of LEE & LOW BOOKS Inc., 95 Madison Avenue, New York, NY 10016.
leeandlow.com

Manufactured in the United States of America

Book design by Carl Angel
Book production by The Kids at Our House
The text is set in Child's Play, Providence Sans, and ITC Stone Serif
The illustrations are rendered in acrylic on canvas

Library of Congress Cataloging-in-Publication Data
Cumpiano, Ina.
Quinito's Neighborhood = El Vecindario de Quinito by Ina Cumpiano; illustrations by José Ramírez.
p. cm.
Summary: Quinito not only knows everyone in his neighborhood, he also knows that each person in his community has a different important occupation.
ISBN 978-0-89239-229-2 (paperback)
I. Title: El vecindario de Quinito. II. Ramírez, José. III. Title.
PZ73.C86 2005   2004065506

20 19 18 17 16 15 14 13 12
First Edition

Special thanks to Laura Chastain and Rosalyn Sheff.